THIS BOOK
BELONGS TO:

_____

DATE RECEIVED: _____

Deep in the ocean, in the coral reef, among the shipwrecks and seaweed, the ocean creatures live and play. Here is what happened to them one warm and sunny day.

Lars was a lionfish who traveled. He would go from place to place looking for other fish in need. When it came right down to it, Lars loved the adventure. Nothing could keep him from his travels.

On this particular day, Lars was looking around for something to eat when he heard a voice coming from below. Lars couldn't quite make out what the voice was saying, so he swam a little closer.

As Lars got closer, he realized the voice sounded frightened. "Please don't eat me!" it said. "I'm only a small guppy and I have no way of defending myself."

"Eat you?" replied Lars. "I don't want to eat you!"

"You don't want to eat me?" asked the guppy, "But you're so big and strong and I must admit, a bit scary."

No one had ever told Lars he was scary.

He could tell what this guppy needed was some courage.

"What's your name little guy?" asked Lars.

"Buster," replied the guppy.

"Well, Buster, I'm Lars. Why don't you come out here and go for a swim with me."

"Out there?" asked Buster. "No way, then someone will eat me for sure!"

"Come on, Buster," said Lars convincingly. "No one out here will touch you with me around."

"Are you sure?" asked Buster.

"You bet I'm sure. You'll be safe and sound."

"Alright. I guess a little swim would be nice," said Buster. With that, Lars and Buster headed out into the big ocean.

As Lars and Buster swam further and further, longer and longer, Buster started to relax. Soon, he was telling jokes and laughing. Buster started telling Lars about when he and his brothers and sisters were just young fry.

Buster talked and swam
and talked. After a while, he
wasn't paying much attention
to where he was going, or
to Lars.

When Buster finally looked
around to see where he was,
he noticed that Lars was
nowhere to be seen.

"Lars, where are you?" called
Buster. There was no answer.
"Lars, I need you!" he called out
again.

"No, you don't," came a voice
from out of the dark. It was Lars.

"Where were you?" asked
Buster angrily. "I was all alone."

"Yes, you were," said Lars.

"I could have been eaten!"
said Buster.